The Right Address

Patricia Gable

Trenton, Georgia

Print ISBN: 978-1-64719-875-6
Ebook ISBN: 978-1-64719-876-3

Published by BookLocker.com, Inc., Trenton, Georgia, U.S.A.

Printed on acid-free paper.

BookLocker.com, Inc.
2021

Dedication

To my granddaughter, Natalie, who helped edit this story
And my writing buddies: Margo, Paula and Diane

Chapter One

January 1985

"Psssst. Willie, wake up," Annie whispered.

Willie was groggy. He pulled the covers over his head.

"Leave me awone," he growled.

"Alone," Annie corrected him, as usual, then shook her head to get back to the point.

"We have to go, Willie. Be very, very quiet. I'll tell you more later."

Annie helped Willie into his winter clothes. Jeans, sweatshirt, boots, gloves, knit hat and coat. She added Willie's shoes to a large black garbage bag, which she had prepared over the last two days. The bag was filled with clothing, shoes, a few books. She put her diary and wallet, with her birthday money in her coat pocket.

She looked around one last time then they tiptoed through the maze of toys and furniture. Nipper, the Warren's cat, leapt to the back of the sofa and let out a high-pitched meow. A signal that he wanted to eat. Annie tossed the cat's favorite toy across the room to distract him.

Hearing the squeak of the bedroom door caused the children to freeze in place. Annie held her breath. A toilet flushing and another squeak of the bedroom door and the house was quiet again. Annie, exhaling deeply, slung the bag of clothes and books over her shoulder and took Willie's hand, leading him out of the front door. They had made it this far at least.

Willie was quiet as they trudged through the darkness and the thin layer of snow. They were walking in the opposite direction they took when walking to school. Farther away from the foster home and anyone who might recognize them. Annie could see the town's lights in the distance, which eased her fear.

"I think I'm hungry, "Willie whined. "Did we have breakfast?"

"No, we didn't. Here's a granola bar." Annie reached in her coat pocket and handed it to Willie.

"Can I sit down to eat it?"

"No, we need to get to those lights," Annie pointed. "Then we will find a place to sit."

They trudged along silently. After what seemed like an eternity, they reached the little town. Most of the store lights were dimmed. One café was open but barely any cars traveled on the main street. Annie searched for a safe place to hide, finding one next to Donna's Diner. A dark alley. They sat in the alley behind a large trash can. That should have been a relief to Annie, but a distant siren made her stomach churn. She remembered something her father used to say, *"No matter how bad things seem, they can always get worse."*

"I wonder if they are looking for us," Annie murmured.

"Who?" Willie asked in a too-loud voice.

"Shh! The Warrens," Annie whispered.

"Are we playing hide and seek?" Willie asked in a softer voice.

"No. We're running away. The Warren's want to separate us, Willie. I heard them arguing again, but this time they were arguing about us. They want me to take care of the baby while they just sit around. They want to send you to a different foster home."

"Was I bad?" Willie's eyes filled with tears.

Annie pulled him closer. "No Willie. You have been very good. But, with the baby, I heard them say they have too much to do and not enough time to take care of us."

The sound of the siren was closer, louder, and Annie put her finger up to her lips so Willie would know to stay quiet. When the police car parked across the street, Annie motioned to Willie to get under the large piece of damp ragged carpeting laying in the alley. She scrambled under the carpet after him. Then they waited.

Annie, hearing footsteps, pulled Willie closer and covered his mouth with her hand. Could the person behind those footsteps hear her heart pounding?

The policeman kicked the trashcan over, scattering rotten food, soiled rags, cans, bottles and coffee grounds. He pointed his flashlight down the alley.

"There's nothing in here," he said.

"Maybe he went to another town," his partner said. "The one just down the road."

"Or maybe…just maybe he is still hiding here in this town. We gotta keep looking. Walk these streets and ask folks if they've seen him. He's so ugly he's hard to miss."

Relief flowed through Annie. She released her grip on Willie, but they remained under the carpet until they could no longer hear footsteps. The alley remained dark, but the street was bathed with sunlight. Annie decided it was time to move.

She did not notice the man standing in the shadows across the street watching them.

Chapter Two

The children stood in the darkest part of the alley and straightened their clothes, brushed off some dirt and waited. Annie was thinking. What next?

She dragged the scroungy carpet into the darkest corner of the alley and shoved their bag of clothes under it. She checked that her wallet and diary were still in her pocket, took a deep breath, and grabbed Willie's hand.

"Willie, when we walk out of this alley, you have to act like we belong here."

"Why?" Willie cocked his head.

"So that no one will know that we ran away from the Warrens."

"Oh. But…"

"Let's see if we can get something to eat." Annie said. She knew that food would distract Willie.

"Goody!"

The stores and coffee shops were beginning to open up. Employees were turning on lights inside, placing the open signs in the windows and sweeping the dusting of snow off of the sidewalks in front of the entrances. The small town's coziness helped Annie relax a little.

At the end of the main street was a gas station with a small store inside.

"Let's get something in there," Annie pointed to the store. "Stay quiet, Willie."

"Can I have a donut?" Willie asked and Annie responded with a squinted glare at him.

They collected a bottle of juice, an apple and a donut each. As Annie paid for the food, the clerk chatted about the weather. Nothing suspicious. The children left the store and found a bench in front of a library.

"Let's have our juice and donut. We can save the apple for later," Annie suggested as they snuggled together to keep warm. Willie's teeth were chattering, and white puffs escaped from his mouth into the cold air.

All the while, Annie was thinking about what to do next, so she didn't notice the man in a black coat standing in the alcove of the library entrance watching them.

"I have an idea!" Annie said, trying to be cheerful. "We can go into the library when it opens."

"Do I hafta do school stuff?" Willie pouted.

"No, we will look at books, use the bathroom and get warm.
The library opened at 9:00am and the children were first in the door. A blast of warm air greeted them. It smelled like old books and fresh coffee. The library was small. As far as Annie could tell, there was only one librarian and one assistant who was shelving some books.

Annie stopped at the librarian's desk with Willie trailing behind her. She puffed up her chest, trying her best to act as old as she could.

"Hello, my name is Annie McDonald, and this is my brother Willie. We came to town because my grandmother is sick, and my mother is staying with her. She said we could come here to read because we were bored at grandmother's house. Is it all right if we stay here without Mother? We promise to be quiet."

The librarian put her glasses on and looked them up and down. "It will be fine if you are well behaved. Any trouble and you will be sent back to your grandmother's. Understand?"

They both nodded sheepishly.
The children's section was in the back corner, decorated with posters and primary-colored tables and chairs. There were

baskets of crayons and pencils on each table and papers stacked by the baskets, some with pictures to color and some blank.

"Annie, can I color?" Willie asked.

She pulled off her knit hat and her dark blond hair spilled out. "Yeah, I'm gonna look for a book."

Annie loved books and found one of her favorites. She returned to the children's area, laid on the carpeted floor and began to read while Willie was coloring.

A girl, wearing a tattered dress, wandered into the children's area. She sat in the corner, leaning against the wall with her book. It wasn't a book for children. Annie noticed the cover, something she had seen before. She wanted to run up to the girl so they could chat about the book. But she knew she couldn't.

What if the girl asked her name? What if she asked where she lived or where she went to school? Annie decided against it.

Hours passed in the peaceful environment. Willie had fallen asleep with his head on the table.

Annie reached in her pocket for her wallet. It was a beautiful leather wallet that her parents had given her for her eighth birthday five years ago. A tear slid down her cheek as she touched the picture of her family that she kept in the front pocket. It was taken on vacation at the beach. Smiles on their faces as they stood by a lop-sided sandcastle that the four of them made. Well, Willie was only two years old, so he wasn't much help. She missed them so much. Why did they have to die? Her birthday money was still in the wallet. She never got a chance to spend it. Now it was money for food.

Pulling her diary out of her pocket, Annie settled at one of the children's tables and reached for a pencil from the basket.

Dear Diary: Today I'm in a library. Usually my most favorite place. But I'm scared. Real scared. We ran away from the Warrens.

She closed the diary. Her hands trembled a little, and she closed her eyes, remembering the first time she had written in her diary. It was an ordinary day when her mother came into her room, sat on the edge of Annie's bed, and handed her a small, wrapped package.

"What's this? It's not my birthday," Annie asked, holding the package.

"No reason, really," Mother replied. "But I have been reading some of your schoolwork and realized that you are not only a good reader but a good writer, too. I thought it would be fun for you to have a place to express your feelings. Private feelings. Good or bad. Funny or sad. The only thing I ask is that you try to write in it every day. Even if it is just one sentence."

She remembered her response. "I promise I will, Mom."

Annie, trying to avoid a gush of tears, got up to use the restroom. As she was returning to the children's area, she caught a glimpse of someone looking through the window. A man. He was tall with dark hair and a grey cap. Was he looking for them? She reflexively ducked her head down as she walked. When she looked up again, he was gone. Did she imagine it?

Chapter Three

Annie and Willie left the library before dark. They stopped at the only fast-food place in town and ordered sandwiches and hot chocolate. It was crowded so no one paid attention to the two runaway children.

Then Annie saw two policemen walking toward the restaurant. It felt like her heart stopped beating. She took Willie's hand and walked over to a group of people who were waiting in line. Their backs were to the policemen. She pushed closer to the group so they could blend in.

"Excuse me," a male voice said from behind them.

Annie held her breath.

"Excuse me, can you hand me some packets of ketchup, please?" the voice asked.

Annie grabbed some of the packets on the counter, and when she turned around, she was face-to-face with a bearded older man. The policemen were sitting across the room talking. Annie breathed again.

It wasn't a long distance to get to the alley but the two walked slowly, tired from the long day. They talked about some of the stores they passed and stopped to look in the window of a unique toy shop. Willie could have stayed there all night, wishing for one thing or another.

When they finally reached the alley, thankfully, the bag of clothing was still there.

"We need to make some kind of bed," Annie said, dragging the rug they hid under last night.

"That rug is too stinky!" Willie pinched his nose and stuck out his tongue making Annie laugh.

"Look, there's a big piece of cardboard behind the trash can. We can use that. I can't remember seeing that last night," she said.

Annie and Willie dragged the cardboard over to the dark corner. They used all the clothes from their bag as pillows and covers.

"The good thing about the alley is that we don't feel the cold wind," Annie said.

"Tell me a story, Annie. Please," begged Willie.

"I'll tell you the story of Corduroy Bear. He's a stuffed bear with green overalls. He got lost in the laundromat and ended up in the washing machine. Lisa, his best friend, was scared when she couldn't find him…"

Soon they were both asleep. And the tall man wearing a black coat watched from across the street, smiling because, as the two children lay sound asleep, the cardboard he left was underneath them.

Chapter Four

"Are we going to the lieberry today?" Willie asked.

"Yes, we are and it's a LIBRARY. "Annie wiped the milk mustache off of Willie's face with her thumb.

They sat on the bench, swinging their feet, kicking the fresh snow on the sidewalk.

"I wish the library was our house," Willie said. "Are we ever going back to the Warrens' house?"

"I don't want to," Annie said gruffly.

"It was better than the old house we lived in. The Clarks. They were mean."

"I know. But I want us to be together and the Warrens want to send you to another foster home. I would miss you." Annie's eyes filled with tears.

"I would miss you, too." Willie hugged Annie's arm.

When they walked into the library, the same little girl was sitting in the corner in the children's area. She was reading the same book she had been reading yesterday. Willie walked over to her, smiled and tapped her book with his finger.

"Who are you?" he asked.

The girl stared at him. No answer.

"Willie, leave the girl alone and go color a picture," Annie scolded.

Annie found the book she was reading yesterday and stretched out on the carpet. Willie was busy coloring-- A sun with a smiley face and some flowers of different colors. Then he stood up and carefully carried the picture over to the girl in the corner. He held it as if it was a piece of glass.

"This is for you," he said proudly.

The girl looked startled but took the picture without a word. Annie jumped up to apologize to the girl.

"I'm sorry that my brother bothered you. He likes making friends."

The girl nodded.

"You are reading one of my favorite books," Annie added, breaking the silence.

A slight smile appeared on the girl's face.

"I like it, too," the girl mumbled.

"The ending of the book surprised me. I had no clue it was going to end like that."

The girl nodded. Her face softened and a slight smile appeared.

"I've read it twice," she said.

"Me, too! Have you read the sequel?" Annie sat down on the floor next to the girl and held up the book she was reading. The sequel.

"Not yet. Is it good?" The girl turned toward Annie.

"Yes! It's really good!"

The two girls excitedly shared their favorite parts of book one. Then Willie plopped down in front of the girls.

"Do you live in this lieberry?" he asked.

Both girls responded at once. "LIBRARY" and then they all laughed.

"My name is Annie, and this goofy kid is my brother, Willie."

“I’m Emma,” the girl replied.

“We don’t go to school now. Do you go to school? I don’t like school. Do you like school?” Willie chattered away.

“I don’t go to school either,” Emma replied shyly and then she added, “But I love school.”

Just as Emma was about to explain why she wasn’t in school, the librarian appeared.

“Emma, your mother is here. Put your book back. I’ll see you tomorrow,” the librarian said.

Emma shrugged into her coat, replaced the book on the shelf and walked away. Then she turned and gave a brief wave to Annie and Willie.

“We should go, too. It will be dark soon. Put your coat on,” Annie said.

The children passed the librarian’s desk and she nodded, a silent “see you later”. She packed up her things and walked to the back of the building to turn off a few lights.

As they walked down the slippery sidewalk, Willie whined, “I need to go to the bathroom.”

"Willie! Why didn't you…oh come on. Let's run back to the library. You can go to the bathroom there."

The door was not locked yet. No librarian at the desk. They quickly walked down the darkened hallway to the bathroom.

"I'll wait out here," Annie said as Willie rushed into the bathroom.

Annie heard the sound of jingling keys and her stomach sunk. "Hurry up, Willie," she murmured.

The keys jangled louder, and then all of the sudden there was the loud click of the door being locked, and, without warning, the lights went out. The hallway was pitch black. Annie could see a dim light at the end of the hall. She opened the bathroom door.

"Willie, are you ok?"

"I'm ok. What happened?" he responded.

Annie gulped. "Well, I think the librarian left. I heard someone locking the front door. We are in here all alone."

Chapter Five

"We can still leave, can't we?"

"I hope so. But what if it sets off an alarm?" Annie rubbed her hands nervously.

They crept down the hall and stood in front of the main doorway.

"See, there's a sticker with the name of the alarm company," Annie pointed. We can't open the door. We don't want the police to find us."

"Call someone. There's a phone on that desk," he pointed.

"Who are we going to call? We sure can't call the police!" Annie was frantic.

"Let's stay here!" Willie spread his arms wide.

"I guess we could. It's warm. We could wash up in the bathroom."

"It's another ah-denture!" Willie danced around in a circle.

"Ad ven ture," Annie said precisely.

They walked slowly around the dimly lit library. It wasn't a very big place. The wooden shelves were polished, groupings of soft chairs were placed in random areas and the librarian's desk was large and orderly. Annie knew that her mother would describe the library as "charming".

When Annie felt her stomach rumble she said, "Let's see if they have a vending machine. I have some change in my wallet."

They were in luck. Two vending machines positioned side-by-side were in a short hallway next to the office of the library director. One with snacks and one with soda, juice and water. They each bought juice and peanut butter crackers.

"Let's sit in those living room chairs," said Willie.

"Sounds good!" Annie replied.

Willie ran ahead of his sister. Just before she passed the front door of the library, she saw a man crouched down looking in the bottom window of the door. Annie backed away from the door and pressed herself against the wall, out of sight. The man jiggled the door to see if it would open. Annie's heart raced, praying that Willie would stay put in the back of the library.

The man walked away. Annie knew it was the same man who was looking in the library window the day before. Dark hair and a black coat. But what is he doing?

After exploring the library, Annie read some books to Willie and by the last one, his eyes were droopy. Time for bed. Well, time for sleeping in a comfy chair. But first she made a diary entry.

Dear Diary: We are locked in the library! Just because Willie had to go to the bathroom. At first, I was scared but I feel safe here. Except there was a man trying to get in, but he went away. It reminded me of a scary movie I saw. But in that one the man really did get in. Also, we met a girl named Emma. So far, I like her, but we have to be careful.

Chapter Six

When the wintery sun peeked through the window, Annie stirred. Her eyes opened; it took her a moment to grasp that she was still in the library. *What a freaky two days it's been* she thought. The best part was that she had a good night's sleep.

"Wake up my little partner in crime," she said, jostling Willie. Willie yawned, stretched and rubbed his stomach.

"I'm hungry."

"Me, too," she said.

Annie dumped the contents of her wallet to see how much money remained. She still had paper money but not much change left. It was early enough for them to get something to eat from the vending machine before the library opened. She hoped the machine took paper money.

"Oh no, the machine only takes change," Annie moaned and started to walk away.

"Look in here!" Willie said.

He was eye-level with the return change chute. His chubby fingers poked around the hole and pulled out quarters, nickels and dimes. Coins tumbled to the floor.

"Way to go!" Annie laughed, but wondered why they hadn't noticed the coins last night.

They had enough change to buy granola bars and juice with money left over. They sat in the cushy chairs and enjoyed their breakfast. Then they gathered the wrappers and juice bottles and threw everything away. They made sure there was no sign of them spending the night there. Willie headed for the children's area.

"Wait, Willie. We should hide in the bathroom. It's almost time for the librarian to get here. We don't want her to know that we have been here all night. We'll wait until we hear other people and then we can walk out and blend in…if we're lucky," Annie reasoned.

They hid in the girl's bathroom stall for what seemed like a year. The flowery deodorizer was so strong it was nauseating. Willie pinched his nose and balanced on the toilet seat, one foot on each side. Annie stood behind him, squished against the wall, with her hands on his shoulders.

Then they heard footsteps. Annie reflexively tightened her grip on Willie's shoulders. Before he could complain, she shushed him.

The bathroom door opened at the same moment a voice came from down the hall. Annie stopped breathing. Willie's eyes widened. Time stopped.

"Mrs. Simpson. Oh, Mrs. Simpson, can you come here for a minute? I need help hanging this banner outside."

Mrs. Simpson closed the bathroom door and turned. "I'm coming!"

Whew…they lucked out. While the ladies were hanging the banner, the children put on their coats and crept out through the side door at the end of the hallway, knowing the alarms were already turned off. They hid in the thorny bushes, damp with a dusting of snow. Annie pushed aside a branch that was scratching her face. Waiting and watching.

When the ladies were back inside, the two waited several minutes. Then they walked in the front door, as if they were just arriving.

"Good morning. How is your grandmother?" the librarian asked.

"About the same," Annie replied. She squeezed Willie's hand as he started to talk.

Emma walked in, distracting the librarian, so Annie and Willie headed for the children's area. Emma joined them.

The three of them sat in a circle whispering. Annie finally asked, "Emma, why aren't you in school?"

Emma looked down, unable to make eye contact with Annie. It was a long time before she spoke.

"My dad left us. Me and my mom. He took all the money. We couldn't pay the rent on the house, so we had to leave. We came to this town. It wasn't very far. Mom knew they had a shelter and she needed to find a job."

"Did she get a job?" Willie asked.

"There's a shelter here?" Annie asked.

At the same time.

"My mom got a job two weeks ago. We are still in the shelter. When she saves enough money, we can rent an apartment."

"What about school?" Annie asked gently.

A tear slid down Emma's cheek. "We don't have an address so I can't go to school yet. Mom became friends with the librarian because we came here a lot in the beginning. The librarian agreed to let me stay here while Mom works. If I'm quiet and good."

"You're lucky! I don't like school!" Willie blurted out.

The girls were quiet, brooding.

Emma finally spoke up. "Why aren't you in school?"

"We ran away!" Willie said proudly.

Emma looked shocked but didn't respond.

"Willie! You can't tell people that. We could get in trouble." Annie flashed an angry look at him.

Then Annie looked at Emma for a long moment before she told their story.

Emma's expression looked as if she was reading a detective novel. Excitement and horror all in one.

"I can tell my mother! She can help you."

"No, no, no! You can't," pleaded Annie. "I shouldn't have told you. Please don't tell anyone."

"But my mom could get you into the shelter. You will get meals and a place to sleep."

Annie shook her head and sighed reluctantly. "Let me think about it."

Then she clutched her diary and moved to a vacant table in the adult section.

Dear Diary: I feel like throwing up. What should I do? Can I trust Emma? I just met her. What if her mom turns us into the police?
Mom? Dad?Give me a sign. Help me figure this out.

Chapter Seven

Willie was coloring a picture at the table; Emma was reading in the corner and Annie returned to the children's area and stretched out on the carpet to read her book. For Annie, it was more like silent staring. Like a ping pong match, her mind was bouncing back and forth. Go to the shelter. Don't go to the shelter. What would be the safest thing to do? Then she remembered something her dad taught her.

She grabbed a pencil and piece of paper from the table and wrote the pros and cons of staying at the shelter.

Pros:

1. They are running out of money so they could get food at the shelter.
2. It would be warmer.
3. They would sleep on a bed or cot.
4. There would be a bathroom.
5. Emma would be there.

Cons:

1. People would ask too many questions.
2. Willie might say the wrong thing.
3. Police or Children's Services might find them.

Annie studied Willie. His clothes were dirty. His white-blond hair was a mess. He coughed a lot when he was sleeping. It would be her fault if he got sick.

Annie got up and sat next to Emma in the corner.

"I've thought a lot about it, and I think I'd like to talk to your mom."

Emma smiled and nodded her head.

An hour later Dana walked into the library, brushed the snow off her shoulders onto the floor mat and headed for the children's area. Emma jumped up and ran to her, grasped her mother's hand and guided her over to her new friends.

"Mom, this is Annie. She loves the same books that I do. And that's Willie. He colored the pretty picture that I showed you. Annie and Willie, this is my mother. Her name is Dana."

Willie jumped up from the table and in one long breath, "Hi! I'm Willie. I can color a picture for you, too. I like to color but I don't like school. Do you like school? What's that thing?"

Dana laughed at Willie, who was poking at the "thing" around her waist.

"It's a fanny pack. It holds my wallet, tissues and my glasses." Dana pulled on the zipper to open it and showed Willie. "This way my hands are free to hold other things or to tickle little boys who ask too many questions!"

Willie gulped and sat down. The girls laughed.

"How was your day?" Dana asked as she sat on the floor facing the girls.

The girls gave her a thumbs up but didn't say anything. Dana studied their faces.

"Are you ready to go, Emma?"

Annie spoke up first. "We…I mean I…need to talk to you."

"Ok, let's talk," Dana swiped her brown hair behind her ear and scooted a little closer.

As Annie began to talk, her voice cracked, holding back tears. She looked down and picked at a random thread on her sweater.

"We were living in a foster home. Actually, we lived in three different foster homes. The last home was ok, but I heard them talking about sending Willie to a different foster home. It scared me. We have to stay together. He needs me…and..and..I need him."

"Can they stay in the shelter with us?" Emma asked.

"Hmmmm, well, maybe for a night or two. But, Annie, people are probably looking for you. The police. The foster parents. School authorities. They are scared, too."

Annie felt worse. If that was even possible.

Dana stood up. "Let's go back to the shelter. We can talk some more and decide what to do."

Annie nodded her head, clutched Willie's hand and lagged behind Emma and her mom. Gritting her teeth, she whispered to herself, "They are not separating us. I won't let them."

Chapter Eight

The shelter was housed in the basement of a church on a side street not far from the library. There was a door in the back of the church and stairs that led to the basement. The foursome stomped on the large foul-smelling rug inside the door to remove most of the wet snow. They followed Dana down the stairs and entered a large room with tables and mismatched chairs and sofas.

Annie quickly counted twelve people in the room. A few people looked up at them. Others continued to read or watch the small television perched on a metal cart. It was so loud that the walls vibrated. One child, about Willie's age, was asleep in a large, overstuffed chair. How could he sleep with the television blaring?

Dana pointed to a small office in the corner. One wall had large windows that looked out to the main room. A man sat at the desk and ran his hand through his dark curly hair as he talked on the phone.

"The guy in there is Brian. He's the director. He is grumpy, so try not to get in his way."

She led them to another room. Triple bunk beds lined the walls. Clothes were spread on some of the beds. Other beds were bare. No sheets or pillows. A closet without a door held boxes, bags and a variety of clothing hanging on a rod the length of the closet.

"This is my bed," Emma pointed to a middle bunk. "Mom sleeps in this bottom bunk."

"You and Willie can use these beds next to us. You can pick bottom, middle or top. No one is using them," Dana said.

"Can I be in the top bunk?" Willie begged.

"Sure, "Dana laughed. "Let's go to the kitchen."

The kitchen was in another large room. Willie's eyes widened when he saw two large refrigerators, two stoves with ovens, and wooden shelves filled with cans of soup and vegetables, plates and cups, baking sheets, pots and pans.

"To be able to stay here we all have chores. Some folks cook and others clean. We wash our own laundry in here." Dana opened a door to a small room, which contained two washers and two dryers.

"Our clothes are in a bag in the alley next to Donna's Diner. At least I hope it's still there," Annie said.

"You two need a good shower. We will find you some clothes to wear for now," Dana said with hands on her hips.

Seeing the bathroom completed the tour. Four sinks, four shower stalls and four toilets also in separate stalls.

"Is this a castle?" Willie asked, causing the others to laugh.

"Willie, when we got here it sure seemed like a castle!" Dana replied. "But this is only temporary. That means that we won't be here for long. This is a place for us to heal. To get better so we can move on in our lives."

Willie nodded but really didn't seem to understand.

Annie had to admit, as she put on clean clothes, that the shower felt amazing. Her curly dark blonde hair hung part-way down her back instead of her usual ponytail. She was grateful to Dana for bringing them here, but she didn't want to get too close to her. She might call the authorities.

The foursome warmed up soup and made grilled cheese sandwiches. Even Willie helped and Annie noticed how happy he seemed. Her guilt surfaced again. She knew running away was hard on Willie.

"So where did you go to school?" Dana asked while they were eating.

“I don’t like school,” Willie answered before Annie could comment.

“We know!” Annie and Emma said at the same time.

“We went to Brookhaven Elementary this year. Before that I was at McKinley and Willie wasn’t in school yet. We moved to a few different schools depending on what district the foster homes were in.”

“I hope that Emma will be in school soon. Maybe at the beginning of next month. I hope there’s a house I can rent that is close to the library.” Dana smiled at her daughter and patted her hand. “I know you miss school.”

“I don’t…” Willie started.

“Like school!” the girls chimed in together. Everyone laughed except for Willie.

After they ate and did the dishes, the foursome played Go Fish on a table in the main room. Brian, the director, stomped through the room and turned the volume down on the tv.

He pointed at a few of the men and said, “I told you guys not to turn the volume up. It gives me a headache!”

He stomped back to his office.

The children went to bed early. Willie fell asleep quickly, coughing now and then as he slept. Annie and Emma whispered back and forth about the books they were reading.

"Ohhhh Annie," Emma whispered. "Jen and Natalie are going to a boy-girl party. I hope she sees John there. He's the one that smiles at her at school. He has dark brown hair and dimples. So C-U-T-E!"

"Oh you're at the good part! They get in big trouble but I'm not going to tell you what happens. In my book I'm at the part when the aliens climb out of the spacecraft. They are funny looking."

Dana shushed them and the girls rolled their eyes, making faces at each other without a sound. Before long the girls fell asleep.

The chore for Annie and Willie tomorrow: taking things to the recycle center.

Chapter Nine

After breakfast Annie and Willie collected bottles, cans and paper within the shelter. They also scoured the church parking lot for recyclables. When the old shopping cart was full, they steered the rusty contraption toward the local recycling shack.

They arrived at the shack and the clerk eyed them up and down. "You new here? I ain't seen you around."

Reacting quickly Annie replied, "We are just visiting. We are helping clean up our grandmother's house."

Willie gave her a puzzled look, ready to say something, but Annie shot him a '*don't say a word*' look and he pressed his lips together.

Next, they pushed the cart to the alley where their bag of possessions was hidden. Luckily, they found it untouched under the cardboard and ragged carpet. Annie heaved the bag into the cart and they headed back to the shelter.

As they walked, Annie saw a man standing by a lamp post on the other side of the street watching them. She recognized him right away… the man who looked in the window at the library and who banged on the library door. And now…

He was crossing the street toward them. Annie's hands gripped the handle of the cart and she walked faster. Eyes straight ahead. Was he with the police? Did he work for Children's Services? Even worse…was he one of those strangers they were always warned about?

She could hear his footsteps quicken as a car horn honked. Footsteps louder, closer. Then the man passed in front of them. So close his open coat brushed the front of the cart. Annie's knuckles were turning white as she held tight to the cart, keeping it between them and the man.

Then the man opened the door of Donna's Diner and walked in.

Annie felt like someone punched her in the stomach. A heart-stopping fear that she needed to set loose somehow. She stopped abruptly to catch her breath.

"What's wrong?" Willie asked.

"Oh, nothing is wrong. I just thought I saw someone that looked familiar. But how could that be? I don't know too many people here, do I?"

"You know me," Willie said.

"And you are the only one that I need to know!" She tousled his clean blond hair.

When they returned to the shelter, Emma was on her bed reading.

"Hey, how's it goin'?" she asked. "My mom just left for work. Do you want to fix lunch with me?"

"I thought you would be at the library," Annie said.

"My mom knew you would be back soon, so she wanted me to wait here for you. Most of the people here don't know you and the director, Brian, can be a grouch," Emma explained.

They ate peanut butter sandwiches, apples and a cookie. Then they walked to the library.

The girls settled in the children's area with their books and Willie was drawing a picture.

Because it was Saturday, other children filtered in and out all afternoon. Annie noticed most of the children made eye contact with Emma and Annie but didn't attempt to make conversation. In fact, Annie thought, they had curious expressions on their faces, and her body tensed.

In this small town, Annie imagined that the children all knew each other. They probably all went to the same school, played sports together and lived in the same neighborhood. They didn't know the three newcomers, Annie, Willie and Emma.

Her mind swirling, Annie worried that the town kids would mention to their parents that they saw unfamiliar kids in the library. What if they started asking questions? She told herself that she was being too suspicious and tried to calm down.

When Dana came to get the children, the librarian asked, "You're taking all three of them?"

Dana shrugged but didn't answer.

Annie spoke up, "My mom knows. She said it would all right if we walk with Dana and Emma to Grandmother's house."

The librarian had a peculiar look on her face but didn't stop them.

Outside, Dana turned to the children, "Let's walk through town before we go to the shelter. I know it's cold but it's sunny and there's supposed to be a storm coming. Lots of snow."

At first, Annie worried that someone would recognize Willie or her. But, she reasoned, we are with Dana and Emma, like a family, so no one would think we were runaways. So, as they walked, her worry faded.

They strolled down the main street, stopped to look in store windows and Dana treated them to hot chocolate in a cozy coffee shop. The smell of fresh coffee and pastries felt like a warm hug. Walls were painted bright orange, green and yellow with black framed posters advertising old movies. The tables were made of dark sturdy wood with grooves, cracks and carved initials.

They talked and laughed about their favorite movies, tv shows, books and music. Warm, comfortable and homelike. More than an hour passed when the group exited the coffee shop. Dana didn't ask too many personal questions. She knew what it felt like to be a "runaway".

Threatening clouds blanketed the sky. A gust of wind tangled Emma's long hair.

"We should head back to the shelter," Dana said, tugging her wool cap down, covering her ears.

Chapter Ten

When they arrived at the shelter, the director Brian, asked to speak to Dana privately. The children went to the bunk room to hang up their coats. Then Annie circled back to try to listen to what Brian was saying.

"Some folks have been asking about those two extra kids that are with you. What's the deal?" Brian had his hands on his hips and a scowl on his face.

Dana started with a nervous laugh. "Well, you know Emma. She has the biggest heart. Emma met them at the library and invited them to stay here so they could play and…" her voice trailed off.

"Where do they live? Why would they want to be **here**? Any parents around?" Brian grilled her.

"I don't really know," she replied quietly.

"Tomorrow's Sunday. By Monday you better give me the answers. I don't like kids!" Brian glared at her.

Dana nodded and walked away.

Annie warmed up a big pot of vegetable soup while Emma and Dana made sandwiches. After eating, they played a rousing game of Chutes and Ladders in the main room. Lots of laughing and clapping from Willie. Then off to bed. Dana didn't mention the conversation she had with Brian.

The next morning, Emma climbed the stairs, opened the door slightly and peeked out to check the weather. The skies were still dark with storm clouds but no snow yet. She scrambled down the stairs to give the weather report to anyone who was awake. A few men and women climbed the stairs and entered the church to join the service. Others watched tv, some were cooking, and a handful were sleeping in the bunk room with the door closed. Overall, a quiet start to the day.

After breakfast, Willie played with the only other boy, Jeff, at the shelter. They found some matchbox cars in a basket of old toys in the closet. In the corner of the main room, they constructed a bridge and some small buildings out of discarded boxes and other found items.

Annie, Emma, and Dana played cards at a table close to the boys. Because it was Sunday, the library was closed.

"Dana, come into my office," Brian called from across the room.

Without responding to him, Dana rolled her eyes at the girls, stood up from the table and walked into the tiny office. There were stacks of papers and folders on the desk and on the tops of two steel gray file cabinets. A map of the town hung on the wall above a bookcase. Brian gestured to the chair and Dana sat down and smoothed her sweater.

"I just got a call from the county sheriff. They are searching for two runaway children. Would you know anything about it?" He glared at her without blinking.

Dana took a long time before she answered. She sat with her hands in her lap and picked at a string on her sweater and didn't look up.

"Yes, I know something about it," she mumbled. "Annie and Willie might be the runaway children, but..."

"Do you know how much trouble you are in? Their parents are frantic."

Dana's head jerked up. "Those people are not their parents. They are foster parents, who are going to separate them," she said forcefully.

"That's not YOUR call!"

"I... I... guess you're right. But what are we going to do?" Dana's chin quivered.

"I will call the sheriff and tell them that we have the runaway kids here. They will probably send a Children's Services person to pick them up."

Dana nodded.

Brian added, "And don't tell them! Don't tell the kids! They may try to run away again. Got it?"

Dana nodded again and walked out of the office.

Emma and Annie were getting restless, so, after lunch they bundled up in their coats, hats and gloves and climbed the stairs.

Emma pushed against the door. "It feels like it's stuck."

Annie joined her, pushing hard, and they both tumbled outside. Into the snow. They had to hold on to each other to stand up. The wind lifted the snow into white spirals dancing in the parking lot and large flakes of snow continued to fall.

"Wow! It's beautiful," Annie said. "I remember when I was little, I would catch snowflakes on my tongue."

They stood a few feet away from the building and stuck their tongues out. Laughing and gathering snowflakes all over themselves except on their tongues. Then they stomped around the parking lot, and when they turned around their footprints were already covered over by more snow.

"We'd better go inside and tell the others about the weather. Maybe Willie and his new friend will want to play out here." Emma suggested.

"Ok, but wait just a second. Listen. It's so quiet and peaceful. Like no one else is in the world." Annie took a deep breath and closed her eyes, taking it all in. Relaxed and happy.

Thirty minutes later, everyone with winter coats came out to check the weather. Trees at the back of the parking lot were bending slightly with the weight of the wet snow. Trash cans had rounded white lids and the few cars on the street were crawling. The two little boys were rolling and wrestling until they looked like miniature snowmen. A few of the men threw snowballs at each other.

Everyone was used to dealing with snow every winter, but this was a lot more than normal and the wind was blowing the snow into large drifts. Gradually everyone had enough and retreated to the warm shelter.

After dinner they played a few more games. Dana watched the children laugh and joke. She did not mention anything about Children's Services or the sheriff's call. Why spoil the day?

Willie climbed up to the top bunk. "I had so much fun today, Annie. Did you?"

Before she could answer, she heard his level breathing and knew he was asleep. She pulled her blanket up to her chin with a book beside her. It was another one of her favorites but, for some reason, she couldn't focus on it. Her mind wandered, thinking of the fun day and the friend she made this week. Emma.

Annie knew that her mom would like Emma. Mom had always paid attention to her friends. She would always tell Annie privately when she was concerned about the behavior of a few of her friends. But Emma. Mom would like Emma.

"I wonder if Emma will still be my friend next week. Or next month," she whispered to herself.

It occurred to Annie that this was the first time she questioned herself about running away. It was the first time she had really thought about the events of the last few days. What are we going to do next? We can't stay here forever. She knew she had no plan. No plan at all.

Annie was fretful all night. Dreaming. Waking. Tossing and turning. One dream was about her mother tucking her in at night, stroking her hair, talking about the day. Another was about Willie sitting on Dad's shoulders when they went for a walk. Still another dream was about the dark alley they slept in. That caused her to sit up in bed. Shaking.

Emma quietly slipped out of bed and stood by Annie's bunk. "Are you ok? Can I help?"

"I'm just having dreams. About my parents and stuff," Annie sniffed but didn't make eye contact.

"I'm so sorry," Emma whispered. "Tell me about them."

The two girls sat cross legged on Annie's bunk. Annie's voice trembled.

"My mom was great. She was a teacher and I used to go in and help her decorate her room and sometimes I would file papers and things. She was real funny, too. Her students loved her. And when I had a problem, she always listened and didn't judge me. In the summer, when she was off, we would go swimming and we had a garden." Annie looked off in the distance, thinking. Remembering.

"And your dad?"

"My dad loved my mom and us. On the weekends we would go hiking or go to a movie. He taught me how to ride my bike. I played soccer and he always came to my games. We built a doghouse together for Max, our dog. He let me paint it by myself. I miss them so much. I think they would be upset if they knew that Willie and I ran away."

They talked quietly for over an hour. Finally, Annie said, "Thanks for listening to me. Whatever happens, I hope we can stay friends somehow."

"Let's make up a friendship handshake!"

They created a special handshake and practiced a few times.

1. High five both hands up high
2. Snap fingers
3. Cross arms and shake hands
4. Uncross and clap twice
5. Fist bump with right hands, then left hands
6. Flat hand on heart

Then Emma climbed back in her bed. Both girls fell asleep.

Chapter Eleven

Annie woke up to the sound of the radio in the main room. She rubbed her eyes and looked around. Willie, Emma and Dana were gone. She scrambled out of bed to find them. No need to get dressed since she slept in a sweatsuit. Most of the residents were gathered around the radio. The reception was scratchy, and the man's slightly frantic voice declared that the town had an emergency. Annie's eyes widened and she froze in place.

Willie sat between Dana and Emma on one of the sofas, and, when he saw Annie, he jumped up and ran to her.

"There's a mergency!" he blurted out. "We are stuck in the snow!"

She took Willie's hand, and they joined the other two on the sofa.

"Everything is closed!" Emma said.

"There's only two snowplows in the town and many of the smaller roads are completely closed. They will be plowing the main street and parking lots first.

"And the fire station!" Willie added.

Just then, Brain came out of his office and motioned to Dana to join him.

"Children's Services will be delayed a few days because of the snow," he told Dana. And again, she just nodded. And again, Annie was watching.

The restaurant where Dana washed dishes was closed, the library and stores were, too. Only emergency locations were open. So, not much to do. Emma helped the two little boys build more things with the empty boxes. A little town for their matchbox cars. They cut holes for windows and doors and used crayons and markers to decorate each piece.

Annie found Dana in the laundry room, tossing clothes in the washer.

"Dana, I need to ask you a question," Annie said.

"Sure, what's up?" Dana replied.

"I noticed that you have been talking with Brian. Is it about me and Willie?"

Dana continued putting things in the washer, checking if pockets were empty, and did not make eye contact with Annie.

"Yes, I talked to Brian. But that's personal, not about you, and not your concern."

Annie stood still, not speaking, waiting for Dana's eyes to meet hers.

"I don't believe you," Annie said in an even tone.

Dana maintained eye contact but did not say anything for a long moment.

Finally, she said, "You're right. It was about you and Willie. Brian asked me not to tell you. The county sheriff called, looking for two missing children. Children's Services will be coming soon to get you. They are delayed because of the storm. I'm so sorry, but maybe it is for the best."

Annie's eyes were moist with tears. "Please don't tell Emma or Willie."

Dana agreed.

Annie went to the bunk room and climbed on her bed. Dana's words echoed in her head "...maybe it's for the best." She had some thinking to do.

"Hey, we've been looking for you! Can you come out and play?" Emma barged into the room, laughing.

Annie laughed, too, trying to be cheerful. They joined Willie and his friend, Jeff, and played with the matchbox cars and the little town they built. Most of the residents were in the main room playing cards, reading and listening to the radio. The television didn't work.

Chapter Twelve

Monday and Tuesday were long days. At least it felt like it. No one could leave the shelter. Nothing was open. Sometimes the kids would go upstairs and look out of the windows to see if anything had changed. It was no longer snowing. By Tuesday afternoon the street was plowed in front of the church but not the parking lot. Someone had shoveled the snow away from the door so they could get out in case of an emergency. But where could they go anyway?

The television worked again so some adults watched tv. Others cooked, read old magazines, napped or did laundry. The kids played hide and seek, but when it got too noisy, Brian told them to find something else to do. Annie and Emma wanted to play "school" with the boys, but they refused to cooperate. So, Annie and Emma climbed in their beds and read their books.

Annie stared at her book, pretending to read, but instead she thought about her conversation with Dana. The words Dana said "*maybe it's for the best*" repeated over and over in her head. What should they do?

"We've come this far," Annie murmured.

"What?" Emma asked.

“Oh nothing. Talking to myself. I was commenting about the book.”

“Is it good? “

“The book? Yes, it’s good,”

Emma rolled over onto her stomach and began reading again. And Annie began thinking again. Should they stay and face the music? Or run again?

Dana came in the bunk room. “Let’s start your chores. There’s a chance we will be able to get out of here for a bit tomorrow.”

Annie found Willie and the two of them gathered cans and bottles for the recycle center. And Annie thought of a plan.

She tossed clean clothes and a book into a garbage bag and shoved it into the bottom of the aging recycle cart. She covered the bag with the bottles and cans they collected. Then she pushed the cart into the closet where it was normally kept.

Her plan was to leave town after they went to the recycle center. She decided that she did not want to be separated from Willie and she did not want to go back to the Warrens. This was her only choice.

But where could they go? She heard people talking about another town several miles away, but with the huge amount of snow it was going to be difficult. Plus, Willie was happy here and he would complain all the way to the next town. The burden overwhelmed her, but she felt she had no other choice.

Chapter Thirteen

The next morning, Wednesday morning, they ate breakfast and put on their winter clothes to go to the recycle center.

"Can I go with you?" Emma asked.

Before Annie could think of a response, Dana cut in, "You can't go Emma. You promised to help me at the restaurant. It might be busy now that folks are looking forward to getting out."

Emma rolled her eyes but nodded in agreement.

Annie pretended to be disappointed but was relieved. Emma would mess up her plan.

The trip to the recycle center took longer than normal. Patches of snow remained on the sidewalks and the cart was hard to handle. But they made it.

"Howdy kiddos!" The recycle man shouted. "You sure have lots of stuff today."

"We been stuck inside!" said Willie. "There was a bizzard."

"I know!" The recycle man laughed and tousled Willie's hair. "It was like a vacation."

"I'd rather be on the beach," Annie said.

The man tipped the shopping cart over and the contents spilled into a pile of cans and bottles. Annie grabbed her trash bag before it ended up in the pile.

They chatted for a few minutes about what they did when they were stuck inside. Then they said their goodbyes, and headed down the main street.

"Can we look in the window at the toy store?" Willie asked.

"Ok," Annie replied. Inside her head a fight was simmering. Was she making a mistake? Should they run or stay? Her jaw hurt from clinching her teeth.

They stood in front of the toy store, gazing at the unique one-of-a-kind toys. Willie was making his "wish list". Then they strolled down the street dodging small piles of snow and other people, who were happy to be outside.

Just then a man raced over to them. The same man who had been watching them. He blocked Willie's path and handed him a card with writing on it. He did not speak and within seconds he was gone.

"What does it say?" Willie shoved the card toward Annie.

Annie's hands were shaking. "It's just an address. 1131 West Market Street."

"He scared me, Annie," Willie whimpered.

She put her arm around him. "It's ok. He didn't hurt us. Maybe he wanted to help us somehow."

A "voice" in her head said, *"Why would you think he was trying to help you?"*

"Let's go back to the shelter. Maybe someone knows where this address is," Annie said.

As they walked, Annie realized that she had made a decision. They weren't running away. Not today anyway.

When they got back to the shelter, Willie's friend was waiting for him to play. They went to the corner and raced their cars around the cardboard buildings and bridges. Annie looked for Dana and found her in the kitchen chopping vegetables for soup.

Annie moved close to her and whispered, "Any news about Children's Services?"

Dana tilted her head toward Annie. “They are coming on Friday unless the weather gets bad again. But the forecast doesn’t call for any storms.”

Annie nodded and went to the bunk room. How could she find Market Street? She remembered that Brian had a town map on the wall in his tiny office. How could she look at it without making Brian suspicious?

Annie had an idea. She found Emma in the kitchen.

Chapter Fourteen

"Hey, I know something fun to do with the boys. Let's have a scavenger hunt!" Annie announced with fake enthusiasm.

Emma shrugged her shoulders. "I guess we could."

"We 'll ask your mom to make a list of things we need to find. Each team will have the same list. And the winner gets an extra dessert!"

"I'm not sure if my mom would do that," Emma seemed skeptical.

"I can ask her! Let me ask her! We need something different to do."

"Ok. I'll come with you," Emma said.

"No, no. I'll take care of it. No problem. It'll be fun. Trust me." Annie skipped away before Emma could respond.

She found Dana laying on her bunk, reading a magazine. She moved her feet when Annie sat at the foot of her bed.

"I need to ask you a favor, but I can't tell you why," Annie said.

Dana raised up on her elbows. "Ok…I think."

"I want you to make a list of things to find, so Emma, the boys and me can have a scavenger hunt."

"Simple enough."

"One of the things I want you to put on the list is to find a street name on the map in Brian's office."

"Ohhhh," Dana shook her head. "I'm not comfortable doing that."

"Please, please. We won't touch anything. We can go in his office when he isn't here. I know it's unlocked because the phone is in there and we would need it in case of an emergency."

Dana looked deep into Annie's eyes for a moment. "This is important to you, isn't it? I can't imagine why, though."

Annie looked down and picked at her thumbnail. "I'm not sure if it's important or not but I need to find out."

Dana nodded. "Ok, I will make the lists and we will wait until Brian leaves. But you're on your own if you get caught in his office."

Dana made the lists for the scavenger hunt before she left for work. She put the papers on her bed and told Emma where they were. Annie sat in the main room pretending to read, but watching Brian's office. He was on the phone.

Emma plopped down next to Annie on the sofa. "Are you ready to start the hunt?"

"No, not yet," Annie answered. "I want to wait until Brian leaves."

"Why?" Emma asked.

"I just don't want him to get mad if we make too much noise."

The two girls chatted for a while and, when Brian left, they heard him tell one of the men that he would be back in an hour or so.

Annie jumped up to find Willie and his friend Jeff so they could start the scavenger hunt. Annie partnered with Jeff and Emma partnered with Willie. They explained the rules to the boys. Then the teams bolted off in different directions.

Jeff was shy, nothing like Willie. But he did know where most things were in the shelter. They found three items quickly: a can of peaches, a magazine picture of a car and a red sock. When Willie and Emma crossed their path Willie bragged, "We found five things so far!"

Annie stuck her tongue out at him and dragged Jeff to another room. She looked at her watch. 20 minutes had passed. She needed to get to Brian's office. They left the laundry room with a flowery smelling dryer sheet, checked it off the list, and headed to Brian's office. Annie's hand was on the discolored doorknob.

"I don't wanna go in that man's room," Jeff said timidly.

"It's ok, Jeff," Annie assured him. "He won't care. We need to look at the map on the wall."

Jeff looked down at the floor and shook his head.

Annie said," Ok, I will go in quickly and look at the map. You stand right here, ok?"

She turned the knob before he could reply. The office smelled like cigarettes and, when she took a few steps, she noticed the floor was sticky. The bookcase in front of the wall map was piled high with folders, papers and books. She stood on her tiptoes to take a close look at the map. She found the library and just two streets away she found Market Street. Not far at all.

"What the heck are you doing in here!" roared the voice behind her, causing Annie to fall back on her heels.

"Answer me!!!"

"I…I…I'm looking for the name of the street where the library is," Annie replied, trying to sound calm.

"You know..." he glared at her. "I don't like you. Or your snotty little brother. You're lucky that Children's Services are coming tomorrow, or I would throw you two out on the street. Now GET OUT!"

Annie left quietly. At least she found what she wanted.

Jeff was waiting in the main room with Emma and Willie.

"Are you ok?" Emma asked.

"Yeh, I'm fine. Brian wasn't happy when he found me in his office. That's all. No problem."

"Did we win?" Willie asked Emma.

"We have everything except the map thing," Emma said.

"You won!" Annie cheered and dropped to the sofa. "We only found six things."

When the boys headed to the corner of the main room to play with their cars, Emma scooted closer to Annie. "Are you sure you're ok? Is there something you're not telling me?"

"Nothing to tell," Annie replied.

Chapter Fifteen

Annie didn't sleep well. She tossed and turned thinking about the man and the address that he had given them. Was it a trap? Should she tell Emma and Dana about it? She was sure that Dana would tell them not to go to the address. But a Children's Services agent was coming TODAY! They may never get a chance to check out the address.

Both girls were quiet as they fixed breakfast. The thought of the Children's Services agent coming depressed both of them. Emma and Annie had become best friends in a short amount of time. They had so much in common. Same age. Same interests. Same turmoil in their lives.

When Willie finished breakfast, he went to look for his buddy Jeff, and Dana left for work. Annie and Emma did the dishes and decided to go to the bunk room to read. But Annie couldn't concentrate. She sat up in her bunk, her legs swinging from the edge of the bed, and faced Emma.

"I need to tell you something," she said.

Emma nodded, closed her book and sat up facing Annie.

“Yesterday when we went to the recycle center, a man approached us. I recognized him because I saw him watching us before. At the library and on Main Street. The thing is, I feel like he isn’t scary or creepy. But I don’t know why. Anyway, yesterday he rushed up to Willie and handed him a card with an address on it. 1131 W. Market Street. And before I could ask the man what it was for, he was gone. “

“What are you going to do about it? You’re not going there, are you?”

“I don’t know what to do. I mean, if I don’t check it out, I may never find out. That Children’s Service lady is coming today to take us away.” Tears trickled down her cheeks.

“Yeh, I’m not sure what I will do without you,” Emma’s voice trembled.

The two girls were quiet, thinking. Then Annie hopped off the bunk and faced Emma.

“Ok, here’s my idea. I’m going to take Willie with me and look for the address. I already know where it is. That’s what I was doing in Brian’s office, looking at the map on the wall. Market Street is two streets away from the library. We need to go soon before the lady comes to take us away.”

“What can I do?” Emma asked.

"You can help by not telling anyone, not even your mom. If someone comes for us, tell them we ran away again, and you don't know where we're going."

"I won't tell even if they threaten to pull out my toenails!" Emma had a way of making Annie laugh even when there was turmoil all around.

"But you will know where we are going just in case…just in case." A worried look spread over Annie's face.

"I'm going to get Willie." She grabbed their winter coats and hats and headed for the main room. She made sure her wallet was in her coat pocket.

She found Willie in the corner with Jeff, playing with their matchbox cars. She tossed his coat to him. "C'mon little bro'. We're going to get some fresh air!"

"Awwww do we have to? Can Jeff come with us?"

"Yes, we have to, and no Jeff can't come," Annie answered in her firm big sister voice.

Brian strolled out of his office and came up behind the kids. "Where are you two going?"

"Just for a walk," Annie answered without making eye contact.

"You know that the people from Children's Services are coming today."

Annie forced a pleasant smile. "Yes, I know. I wanted Willie to get some exercise and fresh air in case we have a long car ride later. He likes looking at the toys in the toy store window."

"Just stay close," Brian scowled, nodded, and walked away.

Annie and Willie climbed the stairs while Willie grumbled, "I don't wanna go for a walk."

They trampled through the church parking lot and Willie pounced into every shrinking pile of snow he could find. Obviously trying to annoy his sister.

She finally turned to him. "Do you remember the card that the man gave to you the other day? Well, we are going to find the address that was on that card."

Willie stopped. Stood still. While Annie continued to walk without him.

"Wait! Slow down! Why are we going there?" Willie ran to catch up.

This time Annie stood still. "If we don't do this now, we may never have a chance. I think there is a reason he gave the address to us. So… let's check it out."

“Ok. Then can we come back and play?”

She didn’t answer.

Soon the steps they took seemed to have more of a purpose as they walked through the small town, passed the library, and turned the corner onto West Market Street. Caught up with curiosity, both children forgot how cold they were.

It wasn’t long before they were standing in front of 1131 West Market Street. It was a two-story white house with dark green shutters and a brick chimney running up the side. Nothing unusual. It seemed to fit in with the other houses on the block. Annie and Willie stood silent for a long time just looking at it.

“Are we gonna knock on the door? “asked Willie.

“I don’t know if…yes, yes we are,” decided Annie suddenly. “Just be quiet. Let me do the talking and if I run, you run, too,” she instructed.

Both children seemed to take a deep breath in unison. Annie knocked on the door. A young woman answered. She looked like she was in her thirties, short stylish brown hair and she clutched a small barking dog in her arms.

“May I help you?” she asked the children.

Neither child spoke.

“Are you selling something?” she asked over the squirming, barking dog.

Again, no answer.

“Look, if I can help, please tell me before my dog has a heart attack,” the woman was laughing.

“Well,” Annie began nervously. “We were walking down the street and there was this man and he gave us this card and it had…”

“That man scared me!” Willie blurted out.

“Well, he didn’t hurt us,” Annie continued with an annoyed glance at her brother. “But he gave us this address.”

She thrust the card up to the screen door which separated them.

This time the woman had no answer. Even the dog stopped barking. Willie and Annie looked at each other and, without saying anything, began to back off the porch.

“Wait,” said the lady and she stretched to look beyond the children. “Where are your parents?

“We are alone,” was all the information that Annie would give.

“But it is so cold outside. Do you live close by?”

"We live in town," Annie replied, which was true. "We don't want anything. Really. We were curious about this card, that's all."

"You know, my dog is usually a good judge of character and he has stopped barking. He must think that you are good people! So, come in out of the cold. You're not afraid of dogs, are you?" The woman was talking as she opened the door.

Annie knew that they should NEVER go in a stranger's house, but Willie rushed in without checking with her first and the dog circled around his feet happily yipping. Annie followed more cautiously as she looked around.

"Please sit down by the fire. It is so cold out there and…" her voice trailed off.

Willie quickly bonded with the dog as Annie and the lady watched. Annie's shoulders relaxed.

"My name is Louise and the crazy dog is Buckeye," the lady smiled and extended her hand.

Annie accepted the handshake and said, "I am Annie and my brother's name is Willie."

"Well relax and I'll get us some hot chocolate." Louise left the room without waiting for an answer.

In the kitchen Louise scurried around fixing sandwiches, fruit, and chips to go with the hot chocolate. Annie heard her humming.

When they were finally settled by the fire, with the food, the dog, and the friendly stranger, Annie felt a heavy weight being lifted.

Instead of bombarding them with questions, Louise talked about the dog and her job.

"I'm the school librarian here in town. Sometimes I take Buckeye to school with me. It's amazing how he settles down when I'm reading a book to the children. The classes I usually have today are on a field trip so I took the day off. A few days ago, we had a few days off because of the storm. Did you see all that snow?"

Willie turned away from the dog and said in a serious voice, "It was a bizzard!"

"Blizzard!" Annie and Louise said at the same time and their eyes met. And they laughed.

"Yeh, one of those," Willie shrugged and turned back to the dog.

It suddenly seemed safe to reveal their story to this woman after being cautious and secretive for so long.

Louise listened without judgement as Annie quietly told the story of how she and Willie left the Warren's home in the middle of the night.

"I heard Mr. and Mrs. Warren arguing, as they did a lot, and Mrs. Warren just had a baby," Annie said. "They were not happy about the baby. They wanted to get rid of Willie and keep me so I could take care of the baby."

Annie's voice got louder, and everything that happened to them spilled out in one long breath. "I could not let them separate us! We only have each other. So, we ran away. We made friends with a girl named Emma in the library. She and her mom live in the town shelter because her dad left them. Emma's mom, her name is Dana, took us to the shelter. So, we got to sleep in a bed and eat hot food and take a shower and we had chores to do. But the director, Brian, he's mean. Well, he got a call from the police looking for two runaway kids. He found out it was us, so he called Children's Services and they are coming today to get us. But then yesterday a man gave us this card with your address. And we wanted to see what it was, like a house or something. So, we told Brian that we were just getting some fresh air and we left."

Annie slumped back on the tan over-stuffed chair and sighed. She released it all. She was drained.

"Oh, my goodness! You are so brave and such a good sister. I am stunned that you have survived all of this."

But before Louise could think things through, Willie jumped up and ran towards a photograph he noticed on the desk in the other room.

“That’s him Annie! That’s the man in the black hat!”

Annie and Louise hurried to the room.

“That can’t be. It’s my husband. He and my son were killed in an accident over a year ago,” Louise whispered as she picked up the framed picture, hugged it close for a moment, then showed it to Annie.

“It’s him. Willie is right,” Annie’s eyes widened.

Suddenly things made sense to Louise. The empty feeling that gnawed at her for over a year was gone. Her eyes moved from picture of the smiling faces of her beloved husband and son to the puzzled faces of the children standing next to her.

Quietly, holding back tears, she said, “Annie. Willie. Let’s sit and talk some more. I think everything is going to be all right. Seems that WE have a guardian angel.

Chapter Sixteen

Back at the shelter Emma sneaked a peek at Brian as he paced the floor waiting for Annie and Willie. She heard him muttering to himself, "I shouldn't have let them leave. I could lose my job."

When he saw her he snarled. "Where are they?"

"Who?" she answered, looking up at him.

"Those two kids. Your buddies. YOU must know where they are. Where they were going. What they are doing. "

"I think they just went for a walk. Willie wanted to look in the window at the toy store. That's what they told me."

"Well, they have been gone too long so they must be doing something else. Tell me!"

Emma calmly looked at his angry face and shrugged her shoulders. "Beats me."

At that moment Dana walked in, returning from work. "What's goin' on?"

"Those two kids are gone. The two kids that you brought here. So, if they don't come back, it's YOUR fault. Your fault for bringing them here in the first place. Those people from Children's Services will be here any minute. What are we gonna do?" Brian paced around nervously.

"I don't know where they are. I've been at work," Dana spoke truthfully. "And watch your tone when you speak to my daughter."

Brian, ignoring Dana, spun around to face Emma. "You know. I know that you know. Spill it young lady!"

Before she could answer, one of the residents appeared at the door. "Some folks here to see you, Brian."

Brian turned pale. He glared at Emma and Dana. Then he left the room.

In the main room stood a policeman, two women and a man. One of the women had a briefcase. Brian put on his "professional face" and extended his hand to the policeman and then to the other man. He nodded to the ladies. "Hello, my name is Brian Simpson, the director here. I hope you had a safe trip."

"Where are they?" asked one of the women. "I'm Mrs. Warren. I'm so worried about my children." Her frumpy clothing, and outdated hair style made her look older than she probably was. And the scowl on her face didn't help either.

"How about a cup of coffee first while we talk?" Brian smiled and gestured to one of the tables. He dragged another chair over to accommodate everyone.

"Where ARE they?" the lady, with hands on her hips, asked again before she sat down.

"Well, the thing is, they went for a walk. To get some fresh air. Willie, that little rascal, likes to look in the window at the toy store. They should be back soon." Brian hustled off to the kitchen to get some coffee for the visitors.

Emma watched through a crack in the bunkroom door as the lady with the briefcase followed him. She was middle-aged with short brown hair. Her forehead wrinkled as she spoke in a firm voice. "I'm Miss Bassitt from Children's Protective Services. You knew we were coming. I don't understand why the children are not here."

Brian fumbled with the coffee pot and filled a few mugs with fresh coffee. All the while, he did not look at Miss Bassitt.

"I've been doing this a long time. I know you are stalling for some reason and I need the truth now." She set her briefcase on the table.

Brian looked defeated. He sunk to a wobbly chair next to the table and dropped his head into his hands. "I don't know where they are."

"Hmmmm. When was the last time that you saw them?"

"This morning. A few hours ago. They said they were going to take a walk."

"Are there any residents here that would have more information? Did they confide in anyone?"

Brian looked up and his face brightened. "There is one resident and her daughter. They were close to the kids. I asked them earlier if they knew anything and they claimed they didn't. Maybe you can get more information out of them. Especially the girl."

"Get them," Miss Bassitt said and walked away. Her high heels clicked on the kitchen floor.

Emma raced back to their bunks to warn her mother that Brian was coming to get them.

Brian entered the bunk room to find Dana and Emma. His hair was rumpled and his voice quivered, "You two need to come with me."

Before Emma could object, Dana gave her a serious look, tilted her head towards the door and they walked into the main room. The volume on the tv was turned down and the four visitors were quietly sipping coffee.

Dana and Emma pulled extra folding chairs over to the table. Miss Bassitt cleared her throat and looked directly at Emma. “We came here to relocate Annie and Willie and they are not here. Brian tells me that you may know something about their whereabouts.”

Emma shook her head. “I don’t know where they are.”

The policeman reached his hand across the table and tapped it in front of Emma, “I think you are protecting your friends. This is very important. If we don’t find them, they could be hurt or lost somewhere. The Warrens have been so worried about them. You need to tell us what you know. Anything that could help us.”

Dana put her arm around Emma’s shoulder. “Sweetie, he is right. What if something has happened to them. Did Annie tell you anything?”

Emma nodded and started to cry. “There was a man…” Mrs. Warren gasped loudly.

“He didn’t hurt them,” Emma said firmly. “The man gave Willie a card with an address on it. They went to find the address.”

Mrs. Warren nearly collapsed in dramatic fashion. “Oh, my darling children.”

Mr. Warren comforted her while Miss Bassitt asked,” Do you know the address?”

Emma bit her lip and looked at her mother.

“If you know, tell them.”

“1131 W. Market Street.” Emma sobbed and ran from the room.

Chapter Seventeen

Willie played with the dog. Whenever he coughed, Buckeye would bark. Willie would lay flat on the floor pretending to sleep and Buckeye would put his paw on Willie's head to "wake" him up. All the while, Annie and Louise shared stories about their families. Anyone watching them would think they had known each other for years. Annie felt warm and safe for the first time in a long time.

Then the doorbell rang. Louise looked puzzled, "This has turned out to be a busy day."

Buckeye, barking, followed Louise to the door. She opened the door to find five people standing there. Two people stood in the front, one of them carrying a briefcase and the other was a policeman! Two adults on the step behind them and one on the sidewalk. And before Louise could greet them, she heard a voice.

"Where are they? "shrieked the woman behind the policeman.

"I warned you!" the lady in the front turned to scold the shrieking woman. Buckeye started barking again.

Annie was sitting in the living room, but she recognized the shrieking voice. Her heart raced. *Mrs. Warren!*

Louise said to the officer in a calm voice, "May I help you?"

"Hello Ma'am, my name is Officer Bill Clark, and this is Miss Bassitt from the Children's Protective Services. We have reason to believe that two runaway children may have come to this address."

Mrs. Warren pushed her way between the two. "Where are they? What have you done with them?"

Just then she caught a glimpse of Willie peeking from behind Louise.

"There you are!" Mrs. Warren squealed and bent to give Willie a hug. But he backed away. The dog growled, baring his teeth.

Annie got up and stood next to Willie with her arm around him protectively.

"May we come in, please? So, we can sort out this situation." Miss Bassitt asked.

"Of course," Louise responded and stood back while the group stepped inside.

The Warrens sat on the sofa with Brian, who never said a word. Miss Bassitt sat on a side chair with her briefcase on her lap and Officer Clark stood. Louise brought in two folding chairs and motioned to Annie to come and sit next to her. Willie and Buckeye sat by the fire.

Miss Bassitt began, "We have been searching for these two children who ran away almost two weeks ago. We tracked them down earlier in the week to a homeless shelter, but the blizzard prevented us from traveling here." She pointed to Brian. "Brian assured us that they were safe in the shelter. But when we arrived today, they were gone, convincing Brian that they were just going to take a walk."

"We found them. Now can we go?" Mrs. Warren demanded.

"No!" Annie replied in a stern voice. "We're not going back with her, and if we are forced to, we will run away again."

Miss Bassitt studied Annie's face and said, "Normally, I would talk to the children privately, but I think we all need to know what's been going on."

"Nothing has been '*going on*'," Mrs. Warren mocked.

Miss Bassitt turned to face Mrs. Warren. "If you don't stop interfering in this conversation, I am sure Officer Clark would love to escort you to the van so you can wait there."

Mr. Warren patted his wife's knee again in an attempt to calm her.

Miss Bassitt placed her briefcase on the floor and leaned forward, facing Annie.

"You're Annie McDonald?" she asked.

Annie nodded.

"Tell me what's been going on, Annie," Miss Bassitt encouraged in a soothing voice.

Annie looked at Louise first, and then back at Miss Bassitt "Well…I heard Mr. and Mrs. Warren arguing…"

"Oh, we never argue," Mrs. Warren said with a forced laugh. "We have discussions."

Miss Bassitt ignored Mrs. Warren. "Go on, Annie."

"I heard them DISCUSSING, which they did a lot. Anyway, they were going to send Willie to another foster home. And I would stay with them to care for their baby."

"Oh, that's nonsense. We would never do that." Mrs. Warren twisted her faded pearl necklace.

"I heard you say it. I'm telling the truth. I can't be separated from Willie. We are family. We are all there is." A tear slid down Annie's cheek. "So, I decided we had to run away."

Miss Bassitt nodded but said nothing.

"We left one night and walked a long way until we got to this town. We hid in a dark alley because we heard a police siren. When it was light enough, we walked to the store to get something to eat. I had money in my wallet from my birthday. Then we went to the library to get warm. We stayed there all day. It was safe."

"How could you do this to me?" Mrs. Warren sniffled. No one paid attention. Miss Bassitt focused on Annie.

"We met a girl, my age, in the library and she and her mother live in the shelter in town. They took us there. We had beds to sleep in and food to eat and chores to do." Annie nodded at Brian.

"Sometimes, during all of this, I saw a man watching us. He wasn't creepy or anything. At first, I thought he was a policeman or a detective or something. Thursday afternoon we took stuff to the recycle center…that was our chore…and the man ran up to Willie and gave him a card with this address on it."

Mrs. Warren sprung off the sofa, "This is preposterous! You are making this up just so you don't get in trouble! I have heard enough! Let's go!"

Miss Bassitt stood. "We are NOT leaving, and I want you to keep your mouth shut."

This time Mr. Warren jumped up. "Don't talk to my wife that way. These children belong in our house."

Officer Clark tried to calm things down between Miss Bassitt and the Warrens, but the voices got louder. He was ready to restrain one or both of the Warrens when he saw Louise jump up and dash over to Willie. He was asleep on the floor by the fire and his cheeks were flushed. How could he sleep with all this turmoil? She felt his forehead and it was hot.

"Willie, wake up, honey," she cooed.

"No. I don't wanna wake up."

"Willie…Willie…wake up." Annie urged as she joined Louise.

"I'll get a thermometer." Louise left the room quickly.

Annie tried to sit Willie up, but he pushed her away. Louise brought a pillow to put under his head and the thermometer.

"You can lay here, Willie. Just open your mouth so I can take your temperature."

They waited.

"It's 103°. I'm going to call my doctor." Louise headed for the phone.

"Wait a minute. We need to take him home so he can get proper care," Mrs. Warren said as she picked up her purse and coat.

"I'm afraid that is not going to happen," Miss Bassitt said firmly. "For one thing, we need to find out what's wrong with him. For another, it's too cold for him to be outside. And, for another thing, we have not decided the best actions for this case. You have not shown any interest in him since we have been here. You may not take him."

Louise came into the room after making the call. "The doctor is a good friend of mine. We went to school together. He is coming over right away. There's a loveseat in the next room. I will put a sheet on it and get some blankets."

When the make-shift bed was ready, Officer Clark carried Willie over and placed him on the loveseat. Louise covered him with a blanket. Annie sat down by Willie's feet. He was still asleep.

"I should have paid attention. Willie has been coughing for a few days, but he didn't seem to have any other symptoms." Annie was close to tears.

"These things can happen pretty fast," Louise assured her. "I will make some coffee for our visitors. Please answer the door when the doctor comes."

The other adults were sitting in the living room. Brian and Officer Clark talked quietly. Miss Bassitt was writing notes in a folder she retrieved from her briefcase and the Warrens were quiet, but Mrs. Warren was nervously tapping her foot on the floor.

Annie went to the door when the doorbell rang, and said to the man at the door, "Hello, I'm Annie. My brother is in the next room."

Louise gave the doctor a friendly hug when he walked in. "Thank you, Ken. I'm sorry to get you out of your warm house."

"No problem. Is this the patient?" He knelt beside Willie. He took his temperature and used his stethoscope.

The doctor turned to Louise and Annie. "Let's get him to sit up and we can check some other things. Hey pardner, I'm Doctor Ken. Can you open your mouth for me?"

When the checkup was complete, Willie fell asleep again and the doctor took Annie and Louise into the kitchen.

"He's a pretty sick kid. I don't have the equipment or meds to help him if he stays here. I suggest that we take him to the hospital to run more tests and get the proper treatment."

Annie sunk to the kitchen chair. "We have no money for a hospital. I should never have dragged him around in the cold."

Louise pulled a chair close to Annie and stroked her hair. "Don't worry about the money. We will get through this."

Annie looked deep into her eyes. "We? You barely know us."

"But I do know you! In fact, my husband knows you, too, and he sent you to me. I want to help you and Willie."

At that moment Miss Bassitt came into the kitchen. "The natives are restless. What's the diagnosis?" She extended her hand to the doctor and said, "I'm Miss Bassitt from the Children's Protective Services."

"I'm taking him to the hospital," Dr. Ken said. "Do you have any of his papers like birth certificate, insurance, known allergies?"

"I may have them in my briefcase and, if not, I will call my office to get the information for you."

Then the Warrens barged into the kitchen.

"What's going on in here?" Mrs. Warren asked loudly.

"Mrs. Warren I'd like you to meet Dr. Ken Holt," Louise replied.

Dr. Ken extended his hand to Mrs. Warren. "Nice to meet you. I'm afraid I can't sit and chat with all of you. I need to get Willie to the hospital."

"Hospital? Whatever for? I think he is faking an illness to get attention. He does that sometimes," Mrs. Warren said.

"Well, he has a high fever and chest congestion. I want to run some tests to see how to treat him."

"Hmph. We can't go with you because we have to get home to relieve the babysitter. Can we just take him with us, and we will call our doctor when we get home?"

Dr. Ken looked at Louise and back at Mrs. Warren. "I don't understand."

"I am his mother," she said in a foul tone and shook her finger at him.

"Foster mother," Annie added.

Miss Bassitt broke into the conversation and faced Mrs. Warren. "I will drive you and your husband home, and as soon as I find out about Willie's condition, I will let you know. When he is better, we will discuss the other situation."

Then she headed to the living room before Mrs. Warren could argue with her.

Mrs. Warren stood still for a moment, thinking. Then she said, "C'mon Annie. Let's go home."

Annie's mouth dropped open. "I'm not going with you. I'm not leaving Willie."

"I believe that legally you must come with me."

Annie did not respond. She rushed from the kitchen and headed to the living room to find Miss Bassitt who was talking quietly with Officer Clark.

"Miss Bassitt, is it a law that I have to go with the Warrens? I want to stay with Willie."

"I will call my supervisor but first let me talk to Louise."

Louise and Dr. Ken were getting Willie ready for the trip to the hospital. Louise held him upright and Dr. Ken raised Willie's arms. He was drowsy but cooperated as they tucked him into his winter coat and hat.

Miss Bassitt spoke in a low voice. "Mrs. Warren wants to take Annie with her. Annie wants to stay with Willie. This is such a strange situation. I know you have not known these children for very long…"

Before Miss Bassitt finished, Louise said, "Annie can stay here with me while Willie is in the hospital. I have plenty of room. Willie needs her to be close by."

"I was hoping you would say that. I will call my supervisor and get temporary legal action for you to keep her here. I know that I have not known you very long, but my gut tells me that you are a good, caring person."

"I can vouch for that," Dr Ken spoke up. "I have known her most of my life."

Annie listened carefully to the adults talking around her and prayed she would be able to stay here with Louise. She did not want to go back to the Warrens ever again. She did not trust that they would keep her and Willie together.

"It's settled then. May I use your phone?" asked Miss Bassitt.

Louise led her to the bedroom., pointed to the phone on the nightstand, and then left to give her some privacy. Miss Bassitt twisted the phone cord with her index finger while she talked privately to her supervisor and explained the whole situation.

Meanwhile Dr. Ken and Officer Clark got Willie into the backseat of the doctor's car. Dr. Ken handed the keys to Officer Clark for him to drive. Coatless Louise and Annie stood by the car, shivering. Annie wrote Willie's date of birth and full name on a piece of paper for the doctor.

"Do you know if he is allergic to any medicines?" the doctor asked.

"No, I don't think he is. He has taken medicine when he has had ear infections and strep throat. No problems," she shrugged.

"Annie and I will come to the hospital as soon as the others leave," Louise added.

Dr. Ken climbed into the back seat and cradled Willie, while Officer Clark drove away, and the other two went into the house. Miss Bassitt was explaining to the Warrens that she received a temporary order for Annie to stay with Louise to be close to Willie.

"Let's get you home to your baby," Miss Bassitt said to the Warrens with an overly cheerful tone.

The Warrens, with scowls on their faces, stood up from the sofa and walked to the door. Then, Mrs. Warren turned and announced firmly, "See you very soon, Annie."

Annie stifled a sob and sank into the nearest chair. Louise dropped to her knees in front of her.

"Look at me, Annie," she said softly. "We need to be strong for Willie. When he gets better, we will deal with the other things. One step at a time. We are in this together."

Annie leaned forward and hugged Louise tightly. Then she nodded in agreement, wiped the random tear from her cheek and stood up. They slipped into their coats, locked the door and climbed into Louise's car.

"Is the hospital very far?" Annie asked.

"No, not far. It's on the edge of town. Not very big but we have good doctors and nurses. Some doctors come from the bigger city a day or two every week."

When they walked in the front entrance, the receptionist recognized Louise. "Hello, Mrs. Shaw. How are you today?"

"Hello Susan. Dr. Ken brought a small boy in, Willie McDonald. Can you check if they are in the emergency room?"

Susan called the emergency room secretary. "Yes," she pointed to the hallway on the left. "Go down that hallway. Dr. Ken will meet you there in the waiting room."

He smiled when he saw them and looked directly at Annie. "Your brother will have some tests. An x-ray of his chest, some blood work. You can sit with him when the nurse draws blood, but not when we take him to a special room to do the x-rays. He will stay tonight at least. I've already requested to get him a room. His oxygen level is lower than it should be. When he gets to his room, we may need to put him on a ventilator."

Annie's chin trembled as she tried to hold back tears. "I wish it was me instead of him. It's all my fault."

Louise took Annie's hand in hers and squeezed it lightly. "Willie seems like a sturdy kid. I think kids often recover faster than adults."

Dr. Ken nodded in agreement. An orderly came to transport Willie to the x-ray room. They watched the bed roll out of the room followed by Dr. Ken, then Annie collapsed into a chair and sobbed. Louise drew her into her arms, held her, and let her cry.

It was a long time before they spoke. Annie, drained of all tears, sat up, and peered into Louise's green eyes. "Thank you, thank you for being here. I don't know how…"

She struggled to think of what to say.

"Oh Annie, you are so welcome. There's no other place I would rather be." She paused then chuckled. "Of course, it would be better if we were at home instead of at the hospital."

Annie smiled, “True.”

Dr. Ken joined them. “Ok, x-rays are completed. Willie is in his room now, so let’s go see him.”

They rode the elevator to the third floor of the three-floor hospital. Room 34. Willie had an IV in his arm and the nurse was preparing to draw blood from the other arm.

Dr. Ken put his hand on Willie’s shoulder. “Willie, you need to wake up for a little bit.”

Willie didn’t move. Annie wished he would open his eyes and ask for his favorite snack. But instead, nothing…no response.

Annie, Louise, and Dr. Ken stood around Willie’s bed. Annie jiggled his arm.

“Wake up Willie,” Annie said with that commanding voice of a big sister.

Finally, Willie’s eyes flickered. He turned his head toward the sound of her voice. Then his eyes widened.

“What?” he grumbled.

“How do you feel?” Annie asked softly, reflexively straightening his blanket.

"Huh? Why?"

He looked around and saw Louise and Dr. Ken staring at him. Then he looked at his arm with the large tan bandage covering the IV needle. His eyes followed the tube up to the bag of clear liquid hanging on a pole.

"Did I have an accident?" Then he began coughing. Deep barking coughs. He squeezed his eyes together in pain.

"You're in the hospital, Willie. I'm Dr. Ken. We are giving you medicine to make you feel better. Where do you hurt right now?"

Willie thought for a moment then rubbed his hand on his chest. Then he wheezed and coughed again.

A nurse came in and stood at the foot of his bed. "I need to check his temperature."

Annie and Louise backed away to give the nurse room to work. Willie opened his mouth and lifted his tongue so the thermometer could lay in the right place.

"It's still 103°, Dr. Ken."

"Check his chart to see if it is time for any of his meds," he replied.

Medicine was added in the IV so that Willie would not have to swallow pills.

Dr. Ken stayed for a few minutes. "Just let him sleep. The nurse will monitor him and answer any questions you have. And I'm only a phone call away."

Annie stared at Willie for a heart- wrenching moment. Then she looked at Louise. "Do you..does Buckeye need to go outside? I mean, do you need to go home?"

"I don't need to do anything but stay here with you," Louise assured Annie. "Let's see if we can get some nourishment and bring it back here and sit with Willie."

The cafeteria was small. A few tables were occupied with folks quietly talking. Looking through the windows, Annie could see that it was dark outside. Flakes of snow clung to the window screen. The parking lot was nearly vacant. They chose steaming vegetable soup, ham sandwiches and two chocolate chip cookies. Louise carried the tray of food and Annie held doors open as they navigated their way back to Willie's room. He was asleep.

The staff had added a second chair and a small table in the room to accommodate the two, knowing they would stay. Louise placed the tray on the table and went to the nurse's station across the hall to get a cup of coffee.

Annie stood by the bed for a moment, bent down and placed a kiss on Willie's cheek. "I'm so sorry little bro," she whispered.

Louise joined her and smiled, "Dr. Ken has already called once to see how Willie is doing. He asked the staff to bring in the extra chair and little table."

They settled into their chairs and began to eat and talk in hushed tones. The nurse came in to check on Willie without waking him. She replaced the almost empty IV bag and checked his oxygen level with a device on his finger. Louise got up to watch.

"This is something new," said the nurse, pointing to the device." Dr. Ken urged the hospital to purchase some of these. It's very helpful in measuring the patient's oxygen level and doesn't bother the patient."

The nurse wrote the findings in Willie's chart and then quietly left the room. Louise returned to her chair and leaned forward. "I have a question, Annie, and if it bothers you just tell me."

Annie nodded.

Louise took a deep breath. "Can you tell me about the encounters you had with my husband when you came to town?"

Annie didn't expect that question. She paused to think. "Well, I began to notice him watching us. One time I saw him looking in the window at the library. And another time he was watching us from across the street. Actually, that happened more than once."

"Besides him watching you, did anything else happen that was strange? He didn't give you anything or do anything else?"

Annie shook her head. "I don't think so. He never talked to us or did anything that would scare us. The only thing he gave us was your address on the card."

They were silent for a while. Annie was trying to recall every detail of the last two weeks. Their time in the alley and the library. The trips to the recycle center. The shelter.

"Hmmmmm, I just thought of something that was strange." Annie sat up straighter.

Louise turned toward her.

"When we were stuck in the library overnight…" Annie began.

"What? You did what?" Louise interrupted.

Annie laughed. A belly laugh. The most she had laughed in weeks. Louise had a blank stare.

"Well.," she took a deep breath. "We spent a lot of time at the library. It was warm and safe. One day, almost closing time, we left the library but then Willie had to go to the bathroom. So, we headed back to the library. The librarian didn't see us come back in, so she locked the door and left. I thought we might set off the alarm, because there was an alarm sticker on the window. I thought if we opened the door the police would come, and Willie convinced me to stay there for the night. The same man…uh, your husband… pounded on the front door and I hid till he left. So, we were hungry, but the vending machine didn't take dollar bills and Willie noticed that there was a bunch of change in the refund opening thingy. And I know those coins weren't in there the day before. And I'm thinking…maybe the man put it in there for us to use. "

Annie collapsed back in her chair and took another deep breath, pleased that she had remembered the incident. Louise stared in stunned silence.

"You have certainly had quite an adventure," Louise finally said. Then she paused, remembering something. "My husband used to collect coins in a jar on his desk."

Annie's eyes lit up. "I remember something else. The first night in the alley we didn't sleep because it was almost morning when we got there. We hid under a stinky piece of carpet. But the second night, we had to make some sort of bed. And there was a big, dry piece of cardboard against the wall that wasn't there before. We slept on top of it and covered up with the clothes we brought in a garbage bag.

Wide-eyed Louise just shook her head in disbelief.

"Do you think it's possible that the man left the coins, the cardboard and the card with your address.?" asked Annie.

"I guess anything is possible. I mean, look what happened when this stranger gave you my address." She shook her head in disbelief.

"Tell me more about your husband," Annie asked.

"My husband, Jack, was a very caring man. He taught math at a school in the next town. And he coached our son's baseball team in the summer. The kids loved him because he made learning fun. Now, I'm thinking, he loved me enough to give me the best gift to help me get through my loss and loneliness," Louise replied.

"You mean us? Me and Willie? We are a gift? We have only been trouble for you!" Annie sprung from her chair.

Louise stood and faced Annie. Her clear blue eyes searched Annie's bleak expression. "Listen to me. When you came to my door, cold and searching, my heart opened up again. I have been in a fog for a long time. Going through the motions in my life. I know... I really know deep down in my soul that we…you, me and Willie... are meant to be a team. A family. So that we can heal and be whole again."

Without hesitation, Annie slid into Louise's open arms and they hugged and cried.

"What's wrong?" a weak voice asked.

Annie and Louise spun around to look at Willie, whose eyes were open. They rushed to his bedside. "What's wrong?" he repeated.

"Nothing's wrong. We're just tired. That's all." Annie smiled up at Louise and then felt Willie's forehead. "You're not as hot today. How do you feel?"

"I dunno. I guess I'm ok," Willie coughed weakly.

"I'll get the nurse to tell her that he is awake," Louise said.

Within a few minutes the nurse and Dr. Ken walked into the room with Louise.

"How you doin?" Dr. Ken asked eagerly.

"Ok," Willie said.

"I'll get his vitals, doctor." The nurse scooted to the side of the bed when Annie and Louise backed away.

Willie cooperated as his temperature and oxygen levels were taken and the doctor listened to his lungs with a stethoscope.

"He is much better," the doctor declared as he looked at the results. "Kids seem to bounce back faster than adults. But I want to keep him here at least one more night to be sure."

Annie's shoulders relaxed and she smiled down at Willie. "You're doing great little dude."

A volunteer walked in with a tray for Willie, which carried jello, juice, milk and a miniature box of Cheerios. She set it on a rolling cart. Then she cranked up the head of the bed allowing Willie to sit up.

"What would you like to eat, Willie?" Louise asked.

"Pizza!" Willie responded eagerly without looking at the tray.

"Well, if he is asking for pizza, he must be ready to come home," said a voice from the open door.

Mrs. Warren strolled into the room with her husband behind her.

Dr. Ken quickly stepped in front of the others. "This boy is not going anywhere."

Mrs. Warren stood with her hands on her hips. "I don't see why not. He is awake, eating and I heard you say that his vitals were good. He can continue to recuperate at home."

"You may have also heard that he is staying here at least one more night," Dr. Ken replied. "And before he goes anywhere Miss Bassitt will make the decision where he is going."

Louise stood next to Willie's bed but said nothing. She opened the carton of milk, poured some on the cereal and handed Willie a spoon. Annie moved next to Dr. Ken.

Mrs. Warren glared at Annie. "You know, you should be punished for running away."

Annie stomped her foot. "And I would do it again!"

"Before things get too heated, you folks need to leave so that our patient can rest," Dr. Ken said as he ushered the Warrens out of the room. He led them to a small sitting room across the hall.

Annie overheard Mrs. Warren whisper to her husband, "Let me do the talking. We need that foster care money. At least for one of them."

Dr. Ken escorted Annie into the sitting room and they both sat down. No one said anything. Mrs. Warren's hands were in her lap and she was looking down. Annie was trembling slightly. Dr. Ken tapped his pen on his tiny notebook. No one spoke for a long time.

"Now what?" Mr. Warren finally blurted out.

Annie suppressed a laugh, surprised that quiet Mr. Warren broke the silence.

"I promise that we will contact you when Willie is ready to leave the hospital," Dr. Ken said. "And we will arrange a meeting with Children's Services to sort all of this out."

"It better be soon," Mrs. Warren replied. "We want these two children back home with us."

"You just want the money!" Annie blurted out.

"That is not true!" Mrs. Warren said indigently.

"Everything will be settled within the next few days," the doctor said, standing up, and ignoring their confrontation.

The Warrens looked at each other and then nodded their heads in agreement. They stood and left the room with no comment to Annie.

Dr. Ken reached over and squeezed Annie's hand.

"We will get through this," he assured her. "I have a few patients to see but I will stop back to check on Willie."

"Thank you so much, "Annie's eyes glistened with tears.

He smiled, nodded and headed down the hall and Annie walked back into Willie's room. He was sleeping. The cart with the half-eaten cereal was pushed away from the bed. Louise was staring out of the window.

"They're gone," Annie said quietly. She stood by the bed and stroked Willie's curly hair.

"That's good. While Willie is sleeping, let's go home and let Buckeye out. We can shower and change clothes. I have some sweaters that may fit you. A little big, probably, but clean and warm."

Annie nodded, kissed Willie on the forehead and followed Louise out of the room.

As they drove the short distance to Market Street, Annie told Louise what happened in the tiny waiting room and how she wanted to laugh when Mr. Warren broke the silence, surprising everyone.

Buckeye was excited to see them. Louise let him out of the back door and they both watched him romp around in the snow before he went to the bathroom. Then Annie took a shower and washed her hair while Louise searched for clothes that might fit her. She found a thick school sweatshirt and sweatpants that belonged to her son and some of her own small sweaters. She placed them on the bed, left the room and went to the kitchen.

When Annie finally came into the kitchen, Louise caught her breath. Here was this girl she had only known for a very short time, dressed in her son's clothes, looking fresh and clean. It should have caused Louise to drop to her knees and sob uncontrollably. But she didn't. She only smiled and said, "You look adorable."

They moved around the kitchen as if it was an everyday occurrence, fixing toast, tea, and fruit. Louise was humming and Annie joined in, recognizing the tune. They ate together and then Annie offered to do the dishes while Louise took a shower. After finishing the dishes, she found a phone book and looked up the phone number of the shelter. She was dialing the number when Louise walked in.

"I'm leaving a message for Dana and Emma. My friends at the shelter. They must be worried about us." Annie explained.

"Good idea," Louise said.

Before leaving the house, Louise filled Buckeye's bowl with food and Annie filled the water bowl. They both grabbed a book and headed to the hospital.

Willie was awake when they walked into his room. The nurse had positioned the cart over his bed, and he was coloring with new crayons and a coloring book. Courtesy of the hospital. He still had the IV in his arm but, luckily, not in his coloring arm.

"Look at YOU!" Annie called out as she strolled to the bed.

"You look different," Willie replied.

Annie laughed and tossed her hair, "I took a shower and washed my hair."

Willie looked at Louise. "I colored something for you, but I can't tear it out of the book. Can you help me?"

"I sure can!" Louise smiled. "We need to hang this up when we get home."

"On the fridgatator?"

"RE-FRI_GER_A_TOR" Louise and Annie said at the same time.

The nurse came in and said," You have visitors. Is it ok if I allow them in?"

Annie and Louise looked at each other. Finally, Louise said, "I suppose."

In walked Dana and Emma. Emma ran to Annie and hugged her.

Dana handed Willie the balloons she brought for him and looked at Louise. "My name is Dana. This is my daughter Emma. We are friends from the shelter."

Louise smiled and took Dana's hand. "I have heard about you both and how much you cared for Annie and Willie. My name is Louise. I'm the one living at 1131 W. Market Street."

Annie and Louise took turns telling Dana and Emma everything that had happened since they left the shelter. Despite everything they had gone through, they laughed as they talked.

After a while, Dana noticed that Willie was yawning. "We had better leave so that Willie can get some rest. But please keep in touch. We miss you so much."

The nurse came in and removed the IV from Willie's arm. She helped him get out of bed and he took a short walk down the hallway. He still coughed and tired easily. When he returned to the room there was another tray of food for lunch. More jello, soup and juice. When he asked for a peanut butter sandwich, Annie knew that he was getting better. After lunch he fell asleep.

In the comfortable silence, both Louise and Annie relaxed and started to read. After an hour or so, they heard a soft knocking on the door. Annie got up and opened the door and found Miss Bassitt.

"Am I interrupting?" she whispered.

"Oh no, not at all. Come in. Willie is sleeping but the noise doesn't seem to bother him." Annie welcomed her.

Miss Bassitt glanced at sleeping Willie and stood in front of Louise. “I was wondering how everything was going. Since he is sleeping, maybe we could go to the cafeteria and chat.”

Louise looked at her watch. “Of course, we can. It’s almost time for an early dinner anyway.”

Annie nodded. They left the room and walked to the cafeteria. Each of them got a tray and chose what they wanted to eat. Then they settled in at a table in the corner by the window. The bright sun was beginning to set, displaying beautiful colors on the horizon.

“Tell me what’s been happening since I last saw you, “Miss Bassitt asked.

Louise told her about the tests they did on Willie to determine that he had pneumonia. Then Annie shared the confrontations with the Warrens, including what Dr. Ken told them.

When they finished catching her up on things, Miss Bassitt said,” We have investigated the Warrens. They have some questionable spending habits with the money they are given for you and Willie. The money is supposed to be for your expenses only. But otherwise, they have had a good record as foster parents. Maybe Mrs. Warren has gotten a little cranky after having the baby. Lack of sleep and all.”

Annie's stomach churned. She gripped the edge of the table, waiting for Miss Bassitt to say that they had to return to the Warrens. She glanced at Louise for support, but Louise looked worried, too.

"Anyway, I talked to my supervisor about this whole situation," Miss Bassitt said.

"I won't go back there!" Annie interrupted.

"Let me finish," Miss Bassitt said. "I know you don't want to go back there. We have a solution. First I need to talk to Louise alone."

"Anything you need to say to me, Annie can hear. I want her to stay," Louise said firmly.

"Ok. Well, how do you feel about being a foster parent to Annie and Willie permanently?" Miss Bassitt stared into Louise's eyes to gauge her reaction.

"YES! Yes. I want to be their foster parent. I really do!" Louise was almost giddy.

Annie clapped her hands and jumped up to hug her.

Miss Bassitt laughed and said, "Annie, I assume this arrangement is all right with you?"

"Yes! Yes! Yes!" she shouted as others in the cafeteria turned to look at her.

"I took a chance and brought the official paperwork for you to fill out, both for temporary and permanent custody. And, we have found someone for the Warrens, too. A troubled girl who needs a home and she loves the idea of helping with the baby."

"That's great!" Annie said.

Miss Bassitt had a puzzled look on her face. "I can't understand how this came together so easily and happily. I've never had a case like this. It was like someone in heaven was handling the whole thing."

"Like a guardian angel?" Annie smiled at Louise.

Two days later, Willie and Annie were settled into their new home. Dana and Emma brought them their clothes from the shelter. Emma helped Annie 'decorate" her own room. It was upstairs with sage green walls and white curtains on the large window. She could see the library in the distance. She had a desk and a velvety forest-green side chair so she could curl up and read.

Willie's room was next to Annie's. He had space to play with his cars on the dark wooden floor. There was a nightstand next to his bed with a lamp shaped like a train engine. One wall was navy blue. The other walls were tan. The curtains were dark red.

Instead of a desk, he had a wooden table with two chairs. On it were crayons and a new coloring book. Dr. Ken came over to check on him and carried Buckeye's bed upstairs and placed it in Willie's room. Buckeye happily curled up in it.

Louise enrolled the two in school, although Willie needed to spend another week recuperating. Annie would be starting on Monday. Nervous but excited. As librarian, Louise had access to the school even on weekends. So, she showed Annie around the school while Dr. Ken stayed with Willie. One wing of the small school was for the younger students. Another wing for middle school and upstairs housed the high school students. The library and lunchroom were in the middle. No gymnasium yet but the playground was large. One section for a basketball court and another for playground equipment.

Sunday afternoon the doorbell rang. Annie opened the door and there stood the Warrens and a girl, a little younger than Annie. Mr. Warren carried the baby, and they all came inside.

"We wanted to wish you good luck," Mrs. Warren smiled. I'm glad it all worked out. This is Adela. She will be living with us now. We were very lucky to find such a sweet girl so quickly. Like magic or maybe a guardian angel watching over us. But we will miss you and Willie."

Louise came in with a big tray of cookies, tea and hot chocolate. She winked at Annie when Mrs. Warren mentioned a guardian angel. Everyone chatted and cooed over the baby.

The doorbell rang again. Louise and Annie looked at each other and shrugged their shoulders.

This time, Louise opened the door. There stood Dana and Emma.

“Howdy, neighbor!” Dana howled as she barged into the house. Emma was laughing but everyone else stared at them.

“What’s going on?” Annie asked.

“Drum roll please…we finally are able to rent a house!” Dana beamed.

“That’s great! Where is it?” Louise asked.

Dana looked at Emma and in unison they said, “Across the street!” They ran to the front window and pointed to the white one-story house. It had black shutters, a bright red door and a big oak tree in the front.

Annie rushed to Emma, hugged her and they both spun around laughing. Then they did their secret handshake.

“We can go to school together!” Emma said.

“It was like a miracle,” Dana said to the group. “A nice man at the restaurant where I work told me about the house. I don’t know how he even knew that I was looking for a place. I hope I see him again so I could thank him."

"What did he look like?" asked Louise.

Dana shrugged her shoulders. "Nice looking. Tall. Long black coat. I think he had dark hair, but he was wearing a grey wool cap, so I didn't see much of his hair."

Louise and Annie shared a knowing look but didn't say anything.

Willie trudged down the stairs rubbing his sleepy eyes. Buckeye trailed behind him. "What's goin' on? I heard someone yell."

"We're happy! Emma and I are going to school tomorrow!"

"Grrrrrr!" Willie growled and started back up the stairs.

"We have cookies down here, Willie!" Louise called to him.

"Yummy!" he came down faster this time. Buckeye inched over to the sofa and sniffed the baby, making everyone laugh.

And the doorbell rang again! This time it was Dr. Ken.

"How's our patient?" He asked while joining everyone in the living room. He patted Willie on the head. "Looks like cookies are the best medicine!"

Everyone talked and made plans for the next few days and beyond. Louise headed to the kitchen and brought back more goodies.

Before she sat down, Louise said, "I am so happy that all of you are here. It's like a celebration for all of us in one way or another. I am especially blessed that I have Annie and Willie."

Willie stood up and added, "Yep, it's all cuz of the garden angel."

And everyone replied, "Guard-i-an Angel!"

Later that night Annie was nestled in her bed, in her OWN room. She thought about everything that had happened over the last two weeks and it made her smile. She reached for her diary, which she had placed on her nightstand.

Dear Diary: I feel so lucky. Willie and I are safe. We have friends, too. I think Mom and Dad would be happy. They would really like Louise. Maybe they even helped our guardian angel. That would be funny. But no matter what...I will always believe in Guardian Angels.

guard·i·an an·gel

/ˈgärdēən ˈˌānjəl/

noun

- 1.a spirit that is believed to watch over and protect a person or place: "the soul was accessible to the gaze of your guardian angel"

Source: Oxford Dictionaries

CPSIA information can be obtained
at www.ICGtesting.com
Printed in the USA
LVHW031354081221
705637LV00006B/264